I0763383

The Book of Lost Magic

The Book of Lost Magic

A JAMS Tale

NEW Reads Publications | Jacksonville, FL

Published in the United States by NEW Reads Publications. NEW Reads Publications is a registered trademark of NEW Reads Publications, LLC in Jacksonville, FL.

newreadspub.com

ISBN 978-1-7357219-6-5 (hardback)
ISBN 978-1-7357219-7-2 (ebook)

Printed in the United States of America

Interior design by Nikesha Elise Williams
Cover design by Erin Kendrick of Erin is Creative

First Edition: September 2022

For the legacy of Augusta Savage and the youth of Duval county—past, present and future—may you dream bigger than the world in which you reside.

CHAPTER 1

The Cummer Museum of Art & Gardens

The sky was warm and sunny as the class walked into the Cummer Museum of Art and Gardens in Jacksonville, Florida. A complete 360 from how the day would soon turn out. From this class, one girl stood out from the rest. Her name was Mira, and she had an immensely strong personality with looks that didn't fit what society called the typical body of a twelve-year-old girl.

Mira's strong personality, defensiveness, and her general treatment of others caused her to get into a fight with a fellow classmate while they toured the Olmsted Garden.

"No one ever understands what I'm going through. All you had to do was listen to me. Ugh," Mira yelled.

This fight was not as serious as it seemed. Mira's sullen attitude was due to the fact she couldn't have control over where the class went to explore in the garden first.

"Ester is always trying to control everything," Mira mutters to herself, continuing the argument on her own. "Why does everything have to go her way?"

Mira really wanted the class and her teachers to feel bad for her. She wanted them to feel guilty and change their minds about what they would explore first.

Unfortunately, she hadn't calculated all the potential possibilities and outcomes. One, they could have just ignored her. Two, they could have changed the location and gone to where she wanted to go, which was what Mira was hoping for. But the last outcome, the real outcome, was completely different.

Mira's classmate Ester snapped at her, "You think you are the only person in this class and every decision has to be made around what Mira wants and not what most of the class wants. You need to learn a serious lesson because your personality will get you in trouble one day."

"You're just mad that your personality is the only thing people like about you because you're ugly." Mira often spoke without thinking about how her words affected others.

She wandered off alone away from the group into the Italian Garden, despite the teacher's orders, causing a scene as she left. Mira kicked up dirt and trampled on the flower beds as her teachers called her name and demanded that she turn around, but she refused to listen.

As Mira walked the Italian Garden, she paced around the fountain ringed in tall shrubbery. Doing laps helped her calm down. She also noticed the atmosphere was different from when she was with her classmates. The bright, sunny day had become darker and frightening, and it was almost hard to breathe.

"Mira, Mira, Mira!" her teachers and classmates yelled. "Where are you?" they called.

Mira heard the voices of the teachers and students looking for her, but she kept walking through the garden, which somehow turned into a dense forest. Even though she was scared, she kept walking, feeling too guilty and embarrassed to go back because of the scene she had caused. Mira couldn't accept being wrong.

She stopped underneath the large Cummer tree. The old oak with its long limbs and massive trunk kept her shaded and hidden as she stared at her reflection in the dark, clear water. So calm and entranced by her own reflection in the water, Mira lost her balance on one of the tree's roots and began to tumble forward. The dark bottom of the reflecting pool began to glow with an intense burning blue light as Mira fell inside. By the time the rest of her class and her teachers got into the garden where she was, she had vanished.

CHAPTER 2

Aeolus, the Kingdom in the Sky

The brash sound of trumpets blew throughout the kingdom filled with wealth and nobility. Golden architecture surrounded everything as far as the eye could see. An assembly of people cheered as the kingdom's army brigade marched carrying the banner flag with the royal family's crest on it. It was a large star with two intertwining lines that met in the middle. With every single wave of the flag, more cheers and applause came from the adoring crowd. Looking from a large watchtower were the prince and princess of Aeolus, the Kingdom in the Sky.

Their names were Kai and Kam. Kai was the cocky and smug prince of the kingdom. Kam was the young but wise-beyond-her-years princess of Aeolus. Their physical appearances gave away the fact that these two siblings were twins. Their grayish-white dreadlocks in matching high ponytails blew as the wind entered the watchtower. A muscular jester paraded along with the army brigade, clutching a salpinx and wearing a hat with white and gold stripes across it. As he marched, he lifted his horn from his side. "Ladies and gentlemen, give it up for your charming, brave, dazzling, and oh-so divine prince and princess of Aeolus. Kai and Kam!"

Kai's body boosted from the watchtower as he performed aerial acrobatics. He ended the show by slamming his fist into the ground. The ground below him crumbled from the impact, as if the foundation was weak. Kam leapt from the watchtower, floating elegantly like an angel down toward the crater her brother had created.

"Can you at least act like you have some sort of common sense?!" she asked through bared teeth.

"Well, excussssse me, princess." Kai grinned at his clearly aggravated sister.

The jester cleared his throat as he spoke to the crowd. "Alright everyone. Now it's time for the best part. The prince and princess will be setting off to a new world! What mysterious creatures will the twins come across?" The crowd was left in suspense as he turned away from them and toward the twins. "So, which one of you will do the honors and open the portal?"

Kai eagerly raised his hand with confidence. "I'll do it," he said. "We don't want Miss Pretty princess to burn through her magic again." He sneered at his sister.

Kam paid her brother's sly comment no mind. Kai hopped off of the cracked concrete and squatted on the ground; he slammed his fist into it, activating his magical powers. A small summoning circle arose from the ground. The blue light coming from the newly opened portal engulfed the entire kingdom.

Kai, full of pride in his abilities, excitedly ran toward the portal entrance. But before he could get even a foot in, Kam grabbed him by the collar of his shirt.

"You know you're forgetting our weapons, right?" she yelled as she yanked him back.

"Oh yeah…oops," he said, embarrassed by his excitement.

Two soldiers walked toward the twins. In the middle of the soldiers was an elderly man. He wore a white robe with gold accents around the sleeves. In his hands, he carried a large chest that he struggled to hold up. The old man stopped in front of the twins and dropped the chest. "Your weapons, my prince and princess," he huffed between wheezing breaths.

Kam opened the chest. Inside of it were two weapons: a two-edged sword with a golden handle and a bow and arrow with a fully stocked quiver. Kai grabbed the sword and put it in a sheath on his back. Kam grabbed the bow and quiver of arrows and secured it with a strap that wrapped around her chest.

Finally, we can get out of this place, Kam thought to herself. I'm tired of looking at the same thing and hearing the same voices every day.

Kai looked at his sister and smirked. He could read her mind and knew all of her thoughts. As they walked into the portal, the elderly man said to them, "Remember: your patches will guide you back home," but by then, the twins had already left, prepared for their new journey.

CHAPTER 3

Pollutio

The world was quiet, desolate, as if the whole place was a library. There was no person in sight in this world that held Earth's waste like a jail. Everyone was hidden in their little houses made of rubble and trash. It was quiet, almost too quiet to hold any living thing that was capable of making a sound. Only for a boy whose aura made sound alone, along with his sharp personality… Bash.

Bash had been living alone since the age of 11 when his mother and father were taken away from him. It left him with no choice but to depend on himself. He went around helping others in hopes they would, in return, offer him something to help him stay alive.

"OH! You're back, son," stated an old man greeting Bash with a smile from ear to ear.

"Yep, I came to see if I could help you with anything," Bash replied.

He hoped the man would have a job for him so he could get some food or some change to get something to eat. The man looked around for a minute, wondering if he had something for Bash to do. Even though Bash had been alone from a young age, he still had the old man that watched over him. The elder taught him one important lesson. The world didn't owe him a thing, so everything he wanted he had to work hard for.

"I do have one job if you are interested. There is one thing, though: this job requires you to go past the trash city into the desert of scraps. When you arrive, look for a sparkly red gem," stated the old man.

"Why do you need a sparkly red gem, if you don't mind me asking, sir?" Bash asked with one eyebrow raised higher than the other.

"Oh, it's just something personal to me that I would like to keep to myself, son," the old man said, turning his big smile upside down to the ground.

"Okay. That's fine. Challenge accepted," Bash said happily, trying to change the old man's mind from whatever he was thinking about.

Bash hurried to his small hut and prepared for the journey to the desert of scraps. The journey would last for three days and two nights, so he would need some things for sleeping and to help him keep warm. The old man gave Bash a map and a staff that had spikes sticking out of the top like a porcupine for his protection. The map had a mark on it to show where the red gem should be located. After getting all his supplies, he began his journey.

I have to make sure I bring back this gem. Maybe I can make the old man proud enough to give me food whenever I need it. When I come back with that red beauty, that old man is not going to believe that I did it all alone. He will want me to be his helper for the rest of his life, Bash pondered, looking forward to his life after coming back with the gem.

He walked for what he believed to be hours. It was getting dark. Engrossed in his daydream, he was finally woken by weird noises behind him. Curious, Bash turned around to see two kids following behind him. A boy and a girl he recognized from his village. They were twins around the age of 10.

"Hey," Bash smiled. "What are you two doing here? You know your parents will be worried, right? You have to go back, even though I would love to have you two join me," Bash said happily to the pair.

The two looked at each other, then to Bash. "Aww man, we wanted to join you on your journey. The old man made it sound so fun." The boy pouted.

"Please, can we join you?" the twins asked at the same time.

"I'm sorry, but you can't come with me. It's too dangerous. I don't want anything bad to happen to you two. You both are like family. Do you guys know the way back?"

The twins shook their heads up and down in unison.

"Okay, well, off you go, and tell your mom and dad I said hi." Bash sent the twins off and continued on his journey. He walked until daybreak and finally made it to his mark. Now all he had to do was look around for the red gem. Searching and searching, Bash saw a bright color, but it wasn't red. The sapphire-colored light source appeared in the sky and it was growing bigger like a stain on a paper towel. Bash was surprised at the sight of another set of twins falling through a bright blue hole. Being careful, Bash hid behind a hill of trash to make sure they were not a threat. Suddenly, right after the twins, he saw a girl fall through a second blue hole in the sky.

"Well, this is interesting." In shock but not forgetting his main purpose, Bash continued on his own, but he couldn't help but be drawn to the new people. Where had they come from? Why were they here?

CHAPTER 4

Falling through the blue light of the portal from Aeolus, Kai and Kam could not see where they were going. The portal opening from their kingdom in the sky had closed. They were cut off from home and unsure of where they were going or where they had ended up.

"Where are we?" Kam asked. "This doesn't look like the realm we are supposed to be in."

The place was full of trash and looked very sketchy and not appealing to the eye. The twins hesitantly took in the new and different world. Curious, they walked around to explore. As they did, they saw a girl, Mira, fall from another portal with the same blue light into the new and strange world. Mira landed face-down in the dirt like a kid falling from a bike. But Kai and Kam didn't notice. They didn't see her fall. They were too focused on the portal. They wanted to leave, so they made a run for the blue light, hoping it would help them get back home.

"No, no, it's closing!" the twins screamed in unison.

On the ground, Mira started to stir. Once on her feet she looked at the twins as if they had committed a murder.

"Yeah, I'm definitely okay. Thanks for checking on me," she said.

Kai and Kam looked from each other to the girl and back. Mira was also confused. As a human from Earth she had no idea about the supernatural, gods, portals, and the magic Kai and Kam had grown up with.

"This is so crazy, but so cool," Mira said in awe. "So I'll forget about you two not helping me."

Kai and Kam looked at Mira curiously. They shrugged their shoulders as the tension quickly lifted as they introduced themselves to one another.

Kai extended his hand and said, "Hi, I'm Kai, and this is my twin sister, Kam."

Mira shook Kai's hand as she said, "Hi, I'm Mira. Where are you from?"

"We are the royal heirs to the kingdom of Aeolus. I am Princess Kam."

"Oh," Mira said, looking down at the ground. "I'm from America on Earth. We don't have any royals there."

Consumed with feelings of insecurity, Mira didn't overreact like she usually would when meeting someone new. Instead of trying to make herself the center of attention and ostracizing herself away from Kai and Kam, she decided to try and get along with the twins. The three of them figured that, since the world was foreign to them, it would be fun for them to go exploring. Mira led the way into the new world. Kai and Kam, just a step behind her, looked at each other with intensity, like they wanted to burn a hole through the other.

"They aren't working, Kam," said Kai.

"What isn't working?" Mira asked curiously.

"Oh, at home we have powers, but ever since we've been here, they don't seem to be working," Kai said.

"I think it has something to do with this realm," Kam added. "But every other realm we've been to, our powers have worked."

Mira's eyes lit up like a Christmas tree when Kai and Kam mentioned their powers.

"This is so cool," Mira squealed excitedly. "Earth is so boring."

The twins laughed at Mira's happiness upon discovering they had powers. They considered her odd to have never experienced the supernatural. What is Earth like? they wondered. Before they could think about it too long, Mira broke into their thoughts.

"Okay, what are we waiting for?" she interrupted. "Let's go exploring."

Mira jumped like a child opening a gift as she continued to lead the way in the new world. Kai and Kam followed behind, trying and failing to tap into the power on the fritz inside of them.

CHAPTER 5

Kai said, "Wow, this place is cool."

The area where Kai, Kam, and Mira stood was shaped like a world made of Lego bricks because of how compact all the trash was. The world was so isolated that on their journey to the city, they didn't see a single person until they finally made it.

There, they saw a boy and a girl who walked past them with smiles that seemed drawn on.

"Hey, you guys from around here?" the girl asked.

"N——..."

Before Mira could finish her sentence, the twins pulled her away from the pair.

"Don't you know not to talk to strangers? They will never have good intentions," the twins said in unison.

"You guys are too serious," Mira said. "It is also rude in my world to ignore people when they speak." She laughed away the twins' cautiousness and walked toward the boy and girl..

"Sorry, guys. No, we are not from here," Mira said. "We are kind of lost and don't know where we are going."

"Oh really… that's cool," the boy said weirdly. "Why don't you guys come along with us, and we can take you somewhere really cool," the boy said after an uncomfortable pause.

Kam tried to decline. "I think we are fine, but thanks."

"Come on, don't you want to have some fun?" Mira asked, jokingly. "I don't think anything bad will happen. Let's just go."

The twins did not want to go with this pair of strangers because they didn't trust people easily. Then again, they also didn't want to ruin the moment. Begrudgingly, they agreed with Mira and decided to follow behind the strange boy and girl who had foreign markings all over their faces.

"Just a little further," said the girl.

The five of them walked for about an hour at least until they arrived at a cave. Even though the sun was setting Mira, Kai, and Kam followed the pair like three baby ducks waddling behind the first thing they saw. Suddenly, the boy and girl stopped in the middle of the dark cave.

"Hey, guys, we are going to have to stop here," the boy said, turning around and abruptly halting his march deep into the cave. "Let's cut to the chase—we really don't care about you having fun. All we want are your things."

Mira, Kai, and Kam looked at each other, confused. Mira was the most confused and hurt. Her face flushed with embarrassment as she realized she should have listened to the twins.

"That's not going to happen," Kai said.

He reached for his sword on his back only to realize it was not there.

"My sword is gone!" Kai roared through the cave.

"Looking for this?" The boy brandished Kai's sword. "You should really be more careful about who you follow."

"How did you? When did you?" Kai asked, trying to figure out when his sword was stolen.

"Yeah. Come on, give me yours! NOW!" the girl demanded of Kam as she stepped behind the boy holding Kai's sword.

Kam took off her bow and arrows and threw them at the girl then backed up with Mira and Kai until they felt an arm around them. Another stranger was behind them. A boy. They immediately jumped away from him, thinking that he was with the pair trying to rob them of their belongings. But he held on to them to reassure them that he could be trusted.

The new stranger said, "Give it back or you'll have to deal with me."

Recognition alighted in the boy and girl's faces as they looked at the stranger who had stepped out to protect them. They threw Kai's sword and Kam's bow and arrows back at them and scampered away.

"Get your stuff," the stranger said.

Kai and Kam reached for their weapons and secured them once again on their backs, never taking their eyes away from the strange boy who'd saved them. Mira waited silently, not knowing who to trust, who to follow, or where to go.

The stranger said, "Guys, come with me. I'll protect you and guide you. I know it might be hard to trust someone else with what's going on, but just follow me."

Desperate, Mira, Kai, and Kam had no choice but to follow behind the new stranger. As they did, he turned to the conniving couple and said, "You can forget about taking their things. They're with me."

The would-be thieves looked at the boy in fear and ran out of the cave.

"Thank you for saving us, but why did you do it?" Kai asked.

"And how do we know we can trust you?" Kam asked.

"First, I will introduce myself," the strange boy said. "My name is Bash, and as you can see, this realm is not your normal realm because it's full of trash, which probably in your realm is seen as abnormal. I've heard of people like you coming to Pollutio before."

"You know who we are?" Kai and Kam asked in unison.

"Why would he know who you are?" Mira asked, with attitude.

Bash rolled his eyes and continued explaining the rules and ways of Pollutio. "In this world, your shiny and new things have no value. The only reason those people wanted to steal your stuff is because, in this realm, stealing is an everyday occurrence. It is our way of life."

"Seems like a crappy way of life to me," Mira muttered.

"Just let him finish explaining," Kam snapped, confronting Mira.

"Thank you," Bash said. "I just want you to know that I don't want your things, and you should know it's going to be hard for you guys to survive alone, so let me help you."

"Why do you want to help us?" Kai asked, eyeing Bash suspiciously.

Mira, Kai, and Kam stared from each other to Bash and back again. Kam's face was the picture of defeat recognizing that they didn't know where they were or really where they were going. Reading her, Kai began to nod his head, accepting that they had no choice but to let Bash be their guide, even though he felt a sinking feeling in the pit of his stomach. Mira watched the exchange between the twins and tried to read their body language. From what she could understand from their subtle movements, she knew that they'd all come to an agreement to let Bash be their guide through Pollutio.

"Okay, we will accept you being our guide," Kam said, begrudgingly.

"But don't try any funny business, okay?" Kai warned.

Mira laughed as they settled differences, not understanding the danger she was about to be in.

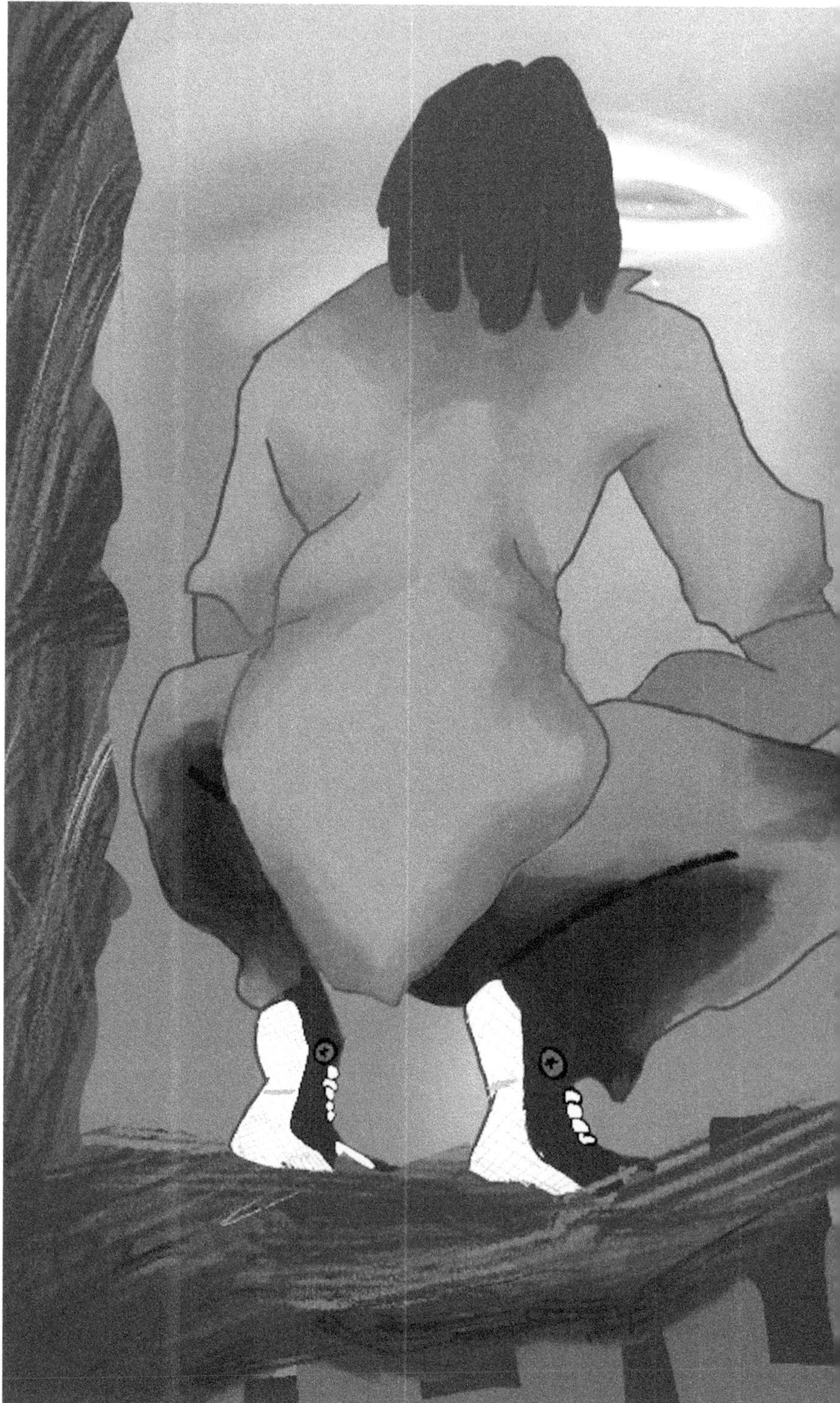

CHAPTER 6

Bash stood in front of a small hut. It was a little broken down with borders around the windows.

"Finally! Home at last!" He shouted, joy flowing through his voice. "Alright, let's head inside," he said.

Bash walked, opening the door to the hut and welcoming the group into his home. Everyone walked in except Mira. Instead, she peered at the interior of the hut in disgust while Kai and Ka followed Bash into the middle of the hut. Mira stayed in the doorway even though Bash began explaining to them more about Pollutio—especially the beast Apollyon.

"The beast has been comin' to this ole place for a while now," Bash said. "He's been terrorizing this place since before I was born."

The twins were stunned by the revelation. "Does this beast have any other worldly powers?" Kam asked Bash, anxiety rising in her voice.

"If ya talking about its magical powers, then yeah," Bash said matter of factly. "One time, that big ole thing burnt down a whole building with just its breath!" he said, turning to face Kam.

So that's why that petrifying feeling has been with us since we got here, Kam thought, using her power of telepathy to communicate with Kai.

Ah, not only that, but our powers have been on the fritz, Kai thought back. But on a more positive note, it seems like when we're far away from the beast, our powers reactivate, even if only a little bit.

Kai and Kam continued their telepathic sidebar.

"So, the Apollyon must also have some magical powers?" Kam assumed. "Is it possible that one of its abilities may be to disrupt any magical energy near its presence or close by to preserve its own?"

Kai said to Kam in his head, That seems to be the case. This ability is in effect when the beast is near anyone else who has magical powers. The further away from it as we can get, the better for us, because the more magic we'll be able to use. Right now, the beast isn't in proximity, so our magic flow is good. But, even with the little bit of power we have, it's not like we'll be able to defeat him.

"Hey, Kam! Hello!" A booming voice invaded Kam's train of thought. She jumped up high into the air, frightened before she realized Bash was speaking to her. Her voice trembled as she said, "Oh, sorry, Bash, can you repeat what you said?"

"Uhh, sure? I guess," Bash said. He repeated the last question of the monologue the twins had missed. "Why do you want the book?"

"Wait, what book?" Kam asked, unable to piece together what Bash had said.

"Ugh, how about you open up those ears of yours!" Bash said, irritation lacing his voice and crisscrossing the smooth planes of his young face.

Mira yelled out loud. In an aggravated tone she said, "The book. Bash is talking about is the book that has some stupid magic writing in it. Apparently the book was located in the town and the Apollyon came looking for it. Blah, blah, blah. He destroyed the town and then took the book with him back to his lair."

Mira summarized what Bash had said about the magical book.

Bash cleared his throat, chuckling nervously. "Yeah, what she said, pretty much. If I remember correctly," he continued, "The Apollyon said something about the book containing some lost or hidden magic. He seemed kinda desperate to get it. I guess he believed that somebody here could use the magic in the book to finally defeat him once and for all, even though no one here knows how to use magic at all. Ha ha." Bash laughed ironically.

"Oh, that book," Kam said, trying to make up for what she hadn't been paying attention to. She pretended to ponder for a moment. "Well, the reason I want the book is because… uh…"

Kam couldn't think of anything to say. She never thought about the book, even with the new information she'd just received. Still, she couldn't come up with a reason she and Kai would need to get the book of lost magic. She figured that even if the book truly contained hidden magical spells, it wasn't like they needed it. They came from a world where magic was always around the corner and always in use.

In Aeolus, there were millions of books, folktales, elders, mages, and witches. That would have all the knowledge they ever needed about magic.

"We want the book because, if we don't help you get it, then the Apollyon will turn this place into his playground and all of you will be his toys, and not in a good way," Kai said, cutting through the silence of Kam's thoughts.

"Oh, that makes sense. Glad to know that you want to help the people of this world," Bash said. He grinned.

"Tch, whatever," Kai said, turning his back to Bash.

"What about you, Mira?" Bash asked, turning to her. "Why do you want the book?"

"Why do I want the book?" Mira asked aloud before pausing for a moment. "Well, you said that the book has magic, and maybe that magic can be used to get me out of this dump and get me back home to Earth." She muttered to herself, "I should have stuck with the group on the field trip at the museum."

Bash didn't hear Mira mumbling to herself. He said reassuringly, "Ah, I'm sure you'll get back to your own world."

"What about you, Bash?" Kam demanded to know. "You've been questioning all of us about our motives for getting this book. What's your reason for desiring the book so badly?"

"Why do I want the book?" Bash repeated. "Ha… that's a long story, but I ran into the Apollyon when I was around the age of seven. I was traveling around, looking at the vast hills of Pollutio's rubble, when I saw some type of black hole pop up. Instead of absorbing things, it spat out the purple beast. He looked a little roughed-up, like he had just gotten into a fight and lost."

Standing in the middle of Bash's modest hut made of compacted, Lego-brick-like trash, Mira, Kai, and Kam listened closely to Bash explain how he watched the Apollyon fall from the sky.

"His eyes were like gems," Bash continued. "They scanned the area before him out of nowhere. Then he launched up and rammed his head into one of the hills of garbage. The hill came crashing down. But that didn't stop her."

Bash paused for a moment in his story as he reflected on the day that his life completely changed. When he went from having just one parent to no parents at all.

Kam zeroed in on the singular detail of Bash's story. Her, she thought to herself. She wanted to know who was this her Bash was referring to. What is her connection to him? Kam continued to ponder about the mysterious woman and what she had to do with the Apollyon. As Kam's thoughts became so engrossed on this one detail Bash shared, she missed many others.

"Ever since then, the Apollyon has taken the book for himself," Bash said, wrapping up his story. "Nothing's happened yet, so I guess he doesn't know how to use it, but we still need to get that book away from him and get you guys back to your worlds."

Mira and Kai nodded their heads in agreement with Bash while Kam looked confused and dumbfounded where she stood, trying to piece together what she missed.

"Alright, so it's settled," Kai said. "The beast has some magical powers we need to work around. Me and Kam will fight him, but with most of our powers on the fritz, it's not a guaranteed defeat."

With the twins unable to access the full range of their telepathy or summon the divinations from their weapons and still untrained on how to control their incantations, they knew they needed to innovate and figure out how to defeat the Apollyon.

Bash said, "I have a few weapons that I made myself. They're not professional, but they'll do something."

"Although this may be futile, Kam and I can hold the beast off. During that time, Bash, you and Mira need to skate by and find the book. Once you two have secured the book, you'll need to escape quickly. We'll try our best to hold the Apollyon back," Kai said.

"So that's the plan," Kam said. "We'll head in, and me and Kai will engage the Apollyon. Bash and Mira can stay back and grab the book."

Everyone seemed pleased with this plan.

"Is everyone ready?" Kam asked, taking charge of the group.

Everyone nodded as they left the hut, prepared to fight the wild Apollyon.

CHAPTER 7

Kai, Kam, Mira, and Bash set out on their journey to look for the book of lost magic in the post-apocalyptic society. The journey on Pollutio was made ten times harder because of the massive amount of compact trash they had to wade through. Surprisingly, Bash lived in a cleaner area of the realm among the trash from Earth that was still as dirty and teeming high as a landfill.

The four maneuvered carefully through the area, looking high and low and around every little hut their eyes could see across the vast land. They were trying to gather clues that would lead them to the book. Eventually, they traveled down a road-like structure made between the mounds of trash by the people of Pollutio. Mira and Bash led the search while the twins followed close behind. Along their journey, Kai, Kam, and Mira spotted a shiny object peeking out beneath one of the mounds of trash. They were intrigued and believed it could be a clue for where the book could be. Believing that maybe the stories of the Apollyon possessing the book could have been false. But Bash wasn't so convinced. He knew from living all of his life on Pollutio that the shiny object they spotted could very well be a trap.

"We don't have time to investigate what that is," Bash said as he tried to keep their search party going where he was leading them.

"Why?" Mira asked, intrigued by the shimmer of the still-unknown object.

"Because it could be a trap. It could cause trouble," Bash said.

Kai and Kam understood Bash's hesitance. They listened to his words and continued to follow him as he walked off, desperate to move away from the object. But Mira, stubborn as she was, didn't agree with Bash. Just like she'd left her classmates in the gardens of the Cummer Museum, Mira dug in her heels and refused to listen to reason. Being her typical self, she decided to move closer and look at the object alone, satisfied in her ignorance to the events that would follow her brazen action.

Closer and closer, Mira inched toward the object until she noticed someone was touching her.

"Mira!" Bash screamed as he hurriedly ran towards her. But Mira was too engrossed in her own mission. Too focused, obsessed with wanting and needing to know what the object was, that she didn't hear Bash yelling her name.

"Why did you pull me away?" Mira shouted at Bash once he reached her. "I almost touched it."

"You can't touch that," Bash said with a frustrated anger present in his voice. "It's too dangerous. You don't know what kind of creature may appear when you touch that thing."

Mira was angry too. She seethed in her feelings like one of the cartoon characters she'd watched as a child on Earth that blew smoke through its ears when mad. She hung back behind Kai, Kam, and Bash, furious over being pulled away from what she wanted to do. I don't care what he says, Mira thought to herself once the three were far enough ahead of her.

Ignoring Bash's warning, Mira turned around and went and pulled the object out to get a better look at it. It looked to Mira like a crushed soda can. She was so engrossed in her investigation of the item that reminded her of home that she didn't notice Kai and Kam turning to each other with horror rippling across their young faces. They saw first what Bash and Mira had yet to see for themselves.

"Mo-mo-mo-mo-monster," the twins stuttered in fear.

Bash turned around as fast as a helicopter propeller and looked at the creature, eye to eye.

"Guys, I want you to run in the other direction and not look back," he said as calmly as possible.

The twins ran off first. Mira sensed the atmosphere had changed around her. She looked up from the object she was holding to see Bash standing between her and the monster. She dropped the object and followed behind Kai and Kam, finally listening to Bash.

With his new friends safe, Bash turned back to the monster, ready to defeat it. But he hesitated. Instead, he had another idea that would involve losing something he had been waiting for for so long. Eye to eye with another treacherous creature, Bash decided right then and there that he was done dealing with the Apollyon.

Satisfied with his decision to not engage in a fight with the Apollyon, Bash rushed to catch up to find Kai, Kam, and Mira. When he reached them, they were back inside his hut. Mira heard the sounds of Bash's heavy boots walking up first. She ran outside, provoked by her anger, still unhappy but this time for a different reason.

"Why didn't you tell me to not touch the object?" she yelled in her outburst. "You could have gotten all of us killed."

Bash clenched his jaw and balled his fists at his side. He was aggravated with Mira's selfishness and angry that not only had she not listened to him, but that she had the nerve to blame others when she decided to act on her own instead of going through with his original plan.

"Mira, you know what? I'm fed up with you!" Bash yelled back at her. "All I have done is try to help you and the twins, and this is how you talk to me? You were the one who could have killed us. You are a very selfish person. You can't even get along with yourself, so I'm done helping YOU!"

Mira, embarrassed to be the target of Bash's anger, stormed off into the realm of trash without saying a single word to the other three. Kai and Kam just looked at each other, unsure of what to do next. Bash stayed put where he was just outside his hut. He was surprised by his own anger and the words that left his mouth.

"Maybe we should go after her," the twins said in unison, after a few uncomfortable moments had passed.

Bash shook his head "no." He refused.

"Let Mira be. Let her cool down and be alone for a while," Bash said.

Kai and Kam had no choice but to agree. They didn't know that Bash had let the monster go free. It was still roaming around, and Bash knew it was only a matter of time before Mira would be taken by the monster. That will keep him busy, Bash thought to himself.

He knew it was important to keep the Apollyon busy because with him occupied with Mira for the rest of the night, Bash would be able to get into the monster's lair to grab the book.

"Guys, I have bad news," Bash said, deciding to let the twins in on his plan. "Mira is going to be taken by the monster from earlier because I didn't defeat him."

Bash hesitated as he watched Kai and Kam's faces go wide with surprise. They looked at him curiously, waiting for him to drop the true reason they'd been feeling unsettled since they arrived.

"I let him go," Bash said finally.

Kai and Kam looked from Bash to each other and back again without speaking. Shock slowly registered across their faces as they realized what he'd done.

We never should have trusted him, Kai and Kam said to each other through their telepathy.

Kai tightened his grip on his sword as Kam reached behind her back for a bow and arrow.

"Stop," Kai said, communicating only with his sister. "He's our only hope."

Kam dropped her arms back to her side, realizing her brother was right. Her face slack and arms loose, she tried not to show the defeat she felt. Instead, she turned from Kai to Bash, feeling resolved about what they needed to do.

"Well, let's go save her," Kam said, ignoring the feeling in the pit of her stomach. "Come on!"

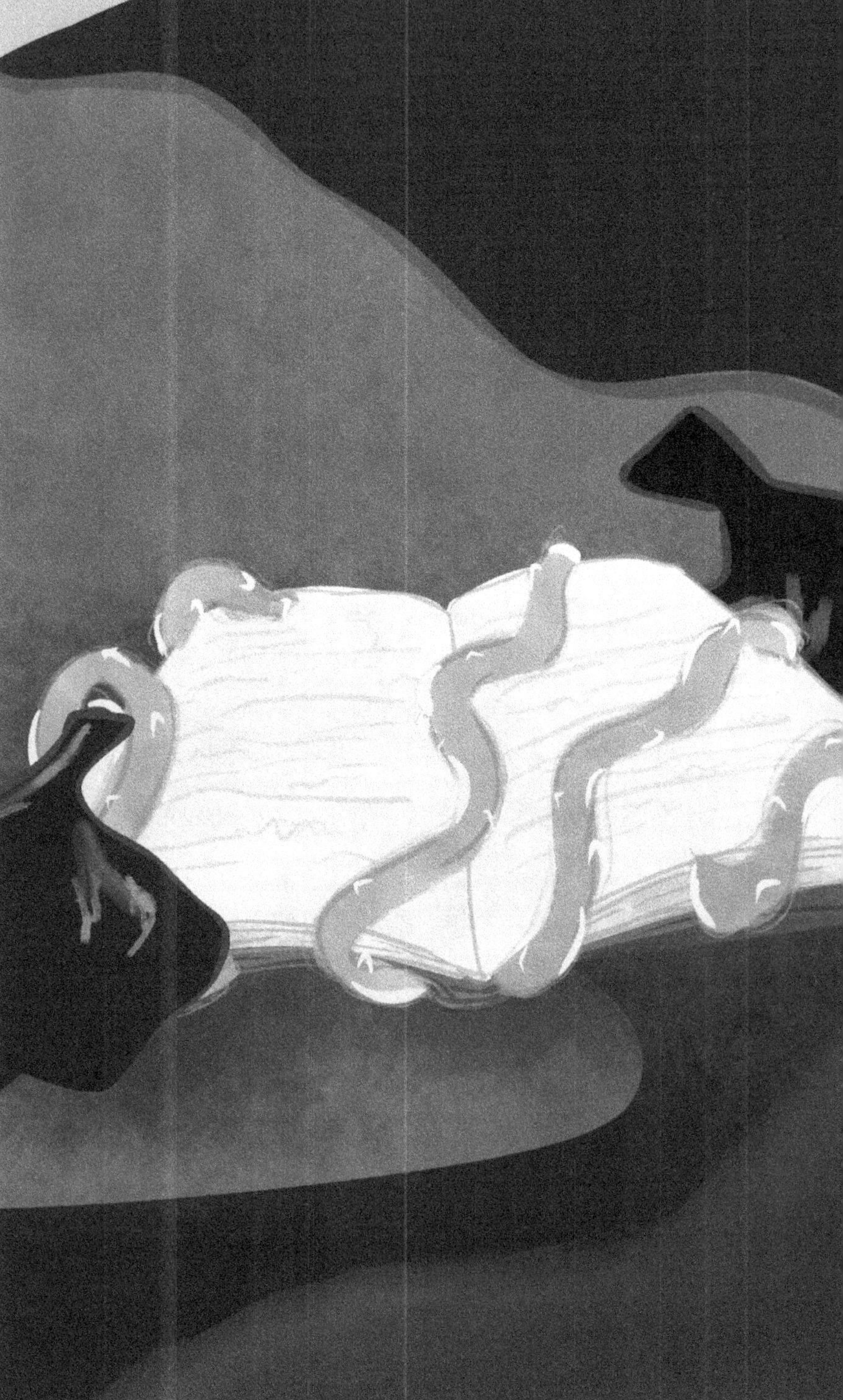

CHAPTER 8

Bash led the way for Kai and Kam. "This way," he said. "We are almost there."

It was late at night as the three walked to the monster's lair to save their lost companion, Mira.

"Do you guys have your weapons ready?" Bash asked. "When we go in the cave, we have to be prepared for whatever may be in there."

Kai held up his sword and Kam gripped her bow and arrows in hand, ready for the attack. Bash had his heavy metal staff ready too. The three of them crept into the cave. The monster was sleeping on the ground next to what looked like its working area, the place where it stored its collected items.

"Hey you, wake up!" Bash yelled. "Where is our friend?"

Kam held her bow ready to aim with an arrow pulled taut, ready to attack. The Apollyon got up like an angry baby being awakened from a nap.

"What is the meaning of this encounter?" the Apollyon demanded to know. "What friend do you speak of? Is it that stubborn girl I captured tonight? Is she the one you speak of?"

The Apollyon, a dark purple beast, was fifteen feet tall, wings on protruding from his back. He cackled to himself. He had two pairs of arms with sharp claws like blades and long creepy eyes that looked like a carnelian. His eyes glowed so bright that they stood out like a sore thumb.

"Where is she?" Kai demanded with his sword drawn, ready to attack. "Where is she? We don't have time for your games. Why did you take her in the first place?"

Kai yelled his barrage of questions at the monster, who just laughed in their faces as he rolled around on the ground of his lair.

"She is being prepared for my dinner tomorrow," the monster managed through its fitful laughter.

"Dinner?" the twins exclaimed in unison.

Bash didn't say a word to the monster. Kai and Kam looked at him as his mind seemed to wander away from the high-stakes encounter with the monster. Instead, Bash looked around the cave for a while until he spotted something of interest. It was the book of lost magic he had mentioned to the twins and Mira.

"Guys, draw your weapons. This conversation is getting us nowhere," Kam said, annoyed with the apparent stalemate. She looked around to see if her brother and Bash were prepared to fight. That was when she noticed Bash standing near the monster's junk.

"Bash, what are you doing?" she yelled. "We have to save Mira first. Her life is more important than the book."

Kai and Kam both looked at Bash with confusion as he ignored them and moved closer toward stealing the book from the monster. The twins watched with their weapons drawn as they tried to keep their attention on the Apollyon to keep him from getting away.

"Guys, the book is more important and will help you get back home," Bash said. He tried to plead his case and explain his actions. "It's right here. Come on." he urged.

"No! We can't leave her." Kai said.

Bash ignored Kai. While the twins had the Apollyon cornered with their weapons, Bash walked over to the collected items in the lair, grabbed the book for himself, and then walked out of the cave.

"We thought we could trust you," the twins cried out after Bash.

They watched as Bash left them, angered and hurt by the betrayal. But they couldn't focus on their own feelings. They twins didn't forget about their mission. They didn't give up on Mira. They understood that they were on their own and they would have to fight the Apollyon anyway.

"Ha ha ha ha." The Apollyon laughed in their faces. "You guys think you can beat me? Think again."

"There is only one way we'll find out," Kai said, ready for war.

CHAPTER 9

The twins stood in their fighting stance, five feet away from the Apollyon. It felt like seconds had turned into minutes, and minutes into hours. It was deathly silent in the monster's lair. They all eyed each other, anticipating who would make the first move. Even the air felt hotter to Kai and Kam, and their bodies began to perspire in places not easily seen. They felt their sweat form, bead, and trickle about their body, insulating them with their own nervous anxiety. Was this because of the dreaded threat looming over them? Were they anxious about the outcome of their battle ahead?

Instantly, the Apollyon cut through the silence and the distance between him and the twins, undeterred by the weapons aimed at his face. With a slash of his arm, the Apollyon struck Kai. Kai's body was flung ten feet backwards through the air from the feedback from the Apollyon's arm. The feedback was so strong that it should have killed him. When he finally hit the ground, he was like a piece of trash being discarded. With his sword shattered into pieces all over the ground, Kai struggled to get up from the attack. His mind raced and his vision seemed to be cut, as if he had gone completely blind. All he could see was white. A strong gust of wind came over him. Kai struggled to catch his breath. It felt as if he was losing oxygen and nothing in his body was working as it should.

"Ah! Ah! Ah!" Kai grunted in agony.

SLAP!

"Pull yourself together!" Kam yelled, her voice full of distress. She had fled away from the Apollyon, ignoring the fact that her backside was exposed. Her focus was solely on her injured brother.

Kai blinked. His vision returned to him, he could see his sister. He launched to his feet, forgetting his pain.

"Kam, we need to do something, and do it quickly!" Kai wailed at Kam.

"You need to stay back and catch your breath. I'll fight the Apollyon myself," she said assuredly.

Observing her twin, Kam noticed that Kai's eyes looked as if they were asking "why," but Kam felt she had no reason to explain herself. Her heart raced. For the first time, she felt weaker than the opponent she was facing. Not only that, she felt the agony her brother was going through. She didn't like the fact that he looked so weak. Kam was afraid that this may be the end for her brother, but there was no more time for her to think about her own feelings.

Kam turned her back on her brother and ran off toward the purple beast. The fifteen-foot distance was nothing for her. With just a few steps, Kam propelled herself forward. Everything in her body was pushing itself to the absolute limit. Her body was like a jet stream as it closed the distance between the purple beast and herself.

Drawing back, the beast prepared to strike Kam with its claw. The claw came down like an axe, but Kam managed to dodge the attack. She prepared an arrow and tried to aim for the Apollyon's gem-like eyes. But the Apollyon possessed the power of intuition. He sensed her attack and used another one of his arms to strike Kam from her side. Her body flew 40 feet into the air. This height should have killed her, but she just barely survived. In mid-air, Kam tried to catch herself, but she was hit by another attack by the Apollyon. She slammed to the ground. The impact caused her body to bounce back up, and she momentarily lost consciousness.

As she started to regain her senses, she noticed that her ears were ringing. It was like a bell had been installed inside her eardrum. Kam tried her best to shake away the sound and maneuver despite the pain she felt. Once she was finally able to stand, Kam limped a little. Her hands were in the position as if she was preparing to shoot an arrow from her bow, but they were empty.

The Apollyon walked towards her, smirking. "Hmm, where's that spunk you just had? Ha ha ha ha!"

The Apollyon looked down on her. Standing at his full fifteen feet of height, he smirked, believing she was nothing more than a fly buzzing around his ear.

Kam had a headache. Her thoughts were focused on nothing but survival. She couldn't give up.

"This may be the attack that ends it all," she heard Kai say behind her.

Kam jerked her head back to see Kai walking toward her and the Apollyon.

"Kam, there's one attack I know will seal the deal," Kai said.

He clenched his fists. Kai's eyes gleamed with determination. His surefire plan was a secret technique passed down from the twins' family. A magical incantation that would override any cursed magic. But there was a cost for using it. They would experience a severe amount of pain because they had not yet learned how to control their ancestral power. It was like a ticking time bomb. Once the fuse was lit, the user willing to speak the incantation had no choice but to commit to the plan. Kai was committed, even though he knew that there had been members of his own royal family who had been completely broken by this technique.

"Are you serious?" Kam exclaimed when she realized what Kai was going to do. "That move is dangerous, and we haven't even learned how to control it."

She completely shut down the idea of using the technique.

Kai was adamant. "I know you're right. This move is dangerous, but I'm not asking you to do it because I know it could completely destroy me. I'm praying for a miracle that may not be heard. I know it's a dream that I can't make come true, but I won't give up," Kai shouted back.

His voice and tone told Kam that he was dead-set on his plan.

"I'm going to defeat the beast, Kam. If you want to stay back, then that's fine. I'll be okay as long as you make it out of here."

Kai had accepted his fate. He knew that if he didn't want the Apollyon to destroy everything, he would have to recite the incantation. Even if it meant his body would be destroyed and he would completely lose his mind.

"I'll bear it somehow," Kai whispered to himself.

He walked away from Kam, marching toward the Apollyon. Kam looked down. She trembled from the top of her head to the soles of her feet.

"Fi... fine," she stuttered. "I won't let you bear that pain alone."

A tear fell from her eye and rolled across her cheek. She ran toward her brother. Catching up to him, she said, "Let's do this together! This was entrusted to us."

Kai looked at his sister. His eyes widened with joy and a smile came across his face. "Right!" he exclaimed.

Kai suggested that they recite the incantation together. Their breathing synced, their heartbeats pounded in time together. Even their sweat seemed to drip down their bodies in anxious harmony as their thoughts aligned. The twins inhaled and exhaled and began reciting the incantation.

Flawless and Firm
Climbing the hill toward twilight's burn

Surviving countless battlefields
Wielding minds and might of steel

Marching onward
Carrying generations
Doubt cast away
We strike with no hesitation

Gaze upon our resolve
Soar into the sky, reaching for Aeolus heavens above

Come forth, our realization
Bind our power in this incantation

In an instant, Kai and Kam's perspective changed to pure white. A strong gust of wind pushed the twins backward, and they struggled to stand up. They couldn't move. Even lifting a finger was a struggle for them. Kam clenched her teeth and tried to push her body forward. Kai clenched his fists and tried to run through the wind. Their efforts were useless. Their vision faded away and the rush of wind ruptured their eardrums. But then they saw it. Through the gust of wind was a golden light. They barely had a glimpse, but the sighting gave them the strength they needed to push through. Their vision fired up, and both of their bodies were cut through by the wind like a giant axe. When Kai and Kam reached the golden light, silence surrounded them. They stood together, their grayish-hair glowing with then golden light shrouding them like halos. Kai and Kam lifted their arms, forcing all of the power of their magic into their arms.

"Ah," they grunted in agony.

The precautions the twins had overlooked came back. Their bodies ached in pain, but they had to push forward. The magical energy flowing from them punished their physical bodies with its recoil. But the twins didn't care. They had no worry. They focused their undivided attention on the Apollyon, who hadn't moved yet but seemed prepared for anything. The Apollyon stared at the twins, full of hostility. It recognized their use of magic.

Moving its eyes, the Apollyon said, "Ho… how… can you two use magic? My presence should dull your senses, quench your powers, and make you incapable of such feats."

The twins did not respond. Then, a huge gust of wind burst from the area. This power wasn't from the Apollyon. It was from the twins. A shape began to form in the twins' hands. The Apollyon was shoved down by the huge gust of wind.

One second.

A ball of golden light formed before them.

Two seconds.

The ball of light formed into the family's crest of a large star and two intertwining lines that met in the middle. Kai and Kam's bodies and mind were constantly breaking, and the surge of energy from the incantation was becoming harder to bear, along with the physical agony the twins were in.

Three seconds.

The Apollyon, who was thrown off balance by the surge of the twins combining power, charged up and dashed up off of the ground. He lifted his massive arm up in the air and prepared to strike the twins down.

Four seconds.

The Apollyon closed the gap, and the twins stepped forward, confronting him. They stood before him, gazing up as he grimaced from his full fifteen feet of height. The muscles of his upper and lower arms flexed. The twins even noticed breath circulating through his body as his windpipe vibrated as he regulated his breathing. At his temple, they noticed a steady tick like a vein pulsing with rage. At their own eye level, all they could see were his legs taut in the stance, ready to attack. The twins took aim at twelve targets and launched the golden star that formed from the glowing golden ball of light in their hands toward the beast.

"Ahhhhhhhhh!" the twins screamed together in unison.

The star jolted forward toward the beast at an incredible speed, striking the Apollyon and hitting all twelve of its targets at once.

"Roarrrrrrrrrrrrr!"

The Apollyon grunted away in agony as the light from the star surrounded its lair. In the light, Kai and Kam could clearly see their surroundings. The image was shocking. The Apollyon remained standing, although his body was severely damaged. His upper arms had been severed off. His lower arms were dangling by the tendons. The magical crest they had launched was strong, but not strong enough. Kai and Kam were dumbfounded. There was nothing else they could do. The magical energy that overflowed through their body had dispersed out of them.

"Ha ha ha!" The Apollyon laughed at the twins. "That one actually stung a little. Good one. Just for that, I think you two deserve a reward."

The Apollyon lifted his torn arm and grabbed the twins. Their bodies were burnt from reciting the incantation, which took hold of them once again and left them both wracked with pain. Kam collapsed in The Apollyon's large claw when he grabbed her. Kai fought to keep his consciousness, but he failed. The twins were defeated by the Apollyon. They too were now its prisoners along with Mira.

CHAPTER 10

Bash sprinted back home, ignoring the howls from Kai and Kam about leaving them to fight the Apollyon. He held the book tightly in his hands until his knuckles turned white.

"Yes! The book of lost magic is mine, finally, after all these years!" Bash said excitedly.

Bash made it back to his hut and quickly sat on his couch, which was nothing more than a few cubes of trash he had put together to sit on. The couch was so wrecked that it was almost coming apart, holding at the seams of the thread he had used to stitch it together.

"I can't believe I got it! After all these years, it's finally in my hands!" Bash shouted at the top of his lungs. "After all these years, Mama, your dream will finally come true."

Thinking of his mom, Bash paused. He gazed at the dusty book in his hand, his mind overflowing with distant memories of his mother. He remembered spending time with her, her smile shining like the rising sun, and her constant generosity always helping the deprived and sickly.

His mother had done her best to make sure everyone experienced an ideal life in such a cruel and unforgiving world. Although she never possessed any riches, her benevolent heart had changed the lives of many with her offerings of food and shelter. Bash thought of his mother until his precious memories nearly overwhelmed his mind. But as he thought about her, one memory stuck out to him like a sore thumb.

Tears poured down from his mother's face, and Bash remembered the tightness that had overtaken his throat and his chest. It was like he was suffocating. His mother was crying over the death of his father; her lover. The rugged world of Pollutio had bared its sharp fangs, and Bash's father died after a long battle with an unknown illness that wracked his body with so much fever and consumption that he rotted from the inside out. Bash and his mother watched his father's decay every day before their eyes. When he finally died, they were both engulfed by their agony.

Bash had watched his mother mourn. He felt helpless. He wanted to do something for the woman who had put everyone else's needs before her own, including his father's. He ran to his mother and hugged her. He tried to offer her comfort the best way he knew how.

"It's okay, mama. You still have me!" Bash recalled saying to her in the wake of his father's death.

But he couldn't keep himself composed. Tears had oozed from his eyes. Instead of Bash comforting his mother, it was his mother who ended up comforting him once again. She set aside all the sorrow she felt for her own loss and gave all of her attention to her son. Bash wondered why she so suddenly seemed to stop mourning her loss. Was it because it was her duty as a mother? Or was it because that was just the kind of person she was? A woman who would give up the world to save one person?

It was only recently that Bash began to ask himself these questions. In thinking about his mother, Bash felt her warmth wrap around him. In that moment, he made it his goal to become just like his mother, to protect those around him and to put a smile on everyone's face. That was who Bash thought he'd become when he was just six years old.

Why? Why? Did I give up on that goal? Bash questioned himself. He tried to find the moment when he had changed. Looking back on his childhood, he realized how idealistic he had been about the world up until his parents died, one after the other. As a child, though he lived in a dump of a world where people needed to rob each other to survive, he believed then that those wouldn't always be his circumstances. With his father dying of sickness and his mother being killed shortly after, he remembered that that was when he began to change.

Now at sixteen years old, he knew the answer to end his struggles and return to his childhood ideals. When his mother had first heard the rumors about a "wish-granting book," she set off to find it for herself. She and Bash explored day in and day out, trying to find the magical book. It didn't take long for Bash to remember why his mother had wanted the book.

"Because if this book can truly grant wishes, Bash, then maybe mama can make this world perfect for everyone," he recalled her saying. "Think about it!

No more stealing others' food. No more looking for spare scraps. No more fighting to live another day. We can all live together in peace!"

Bash remembered the excitement his mother's voice had held. It burst through her and radiated throughout her entire body. That was why she didn't back down from the Apollyon when she had encountered it. The book had been right there in a field near the Apollyons's lair. Her goal, her dream, her desire was right there, and she was so close to it. Only the Apollyon stood in her way. And although the mighty beast stood in front of her, she was not willing to back down.

In the field filled with hills of scraps, the Apollyon and Bash's mother fought. The Apollyon knocked over a hill. Bash's mother shoved him away from the falling mountain of trash, sacrificing herself to save him.

Bash shook his head to clear the memories of his mother's final moments, her last act in service to another. To him.

Sitting on the couch in his hut, Bash stared at the book of lost magic. Tears gushed from his eyes. He was choked up, thinking about his mother's sacrifice and how he had so easily given up on his friends for his selfish goal. Bash knew that his mother never would have sacrificed anyone else for her own greed.

"Mama, your dream was to make a perfect world," Bash said aloud. "Well, a world without my friends is a terrible world."

Bash stood up from the couch, walked to the side of his hut, and grabbed two staffs made of disposed scraps. He put them in the back of his shirt and threw the book down.

"I'm coming, y'all!" Bash yelled.

He dashed out of his hut. His mind was set on saving his friends no matter what. He ran all the way to the Apollyon's lair, ready for the final battle.

"I'm such an idiot. Why did I do that?" He questioned himself on his journey. "I shouldn't have left the twins and Mira in the cave with that monster. Even if they are warriors, they are not used to the evils of this world, but I am!"

Nearing the Apollyon's cave, Bash shouted aloud to himself, "Hope you guys can forgive me after this!" He hoped his words would make it all the way to Kai, Kam and Mira.

CHAPTER 11

Mira kicked the prison cell wall and let out a frustrated growl before plopping down into a corner, pouting.

"Ugh!" she moaned. "This is all their fault! If they had only listened to me, none of this would've happened!" She punched the wall beside her with the side of her fist. "Maybe if the twins weren't so reckless... maybe if Bash wasn't such a— wait. Bash. It's his fault! He sold us out to the monster! That little —"

Mira could feel a sense of anger, frustration, and betrayal flowing through her. She felt her face get hot with rage. She kicked around the dirt and rubble and threw a temper tantrum like she always did when she was home and didn't get her way on Earth. She continued with her irrational outburst for nearly ten minutes, but to her it felt like thirty seconds. When she finally settled down, she plopped back down into her little corner, realizing there was nothing she could do. She was trapped in a cell. A prisoner in the Apollyon's lair. Mira closed her eyes and sighed.

Why did this have to happen to me? Mira thought to herself. She began to think about how she might be able to get out of the prison cell. Instead, she was besieged by thoughts and memories of her own bad behavior.

Was I a little ungrateful? Yes. Was I bratty? Yes. Was I rude? Yes. But do I deserve to be locked up in a dark cell, threatened by a monster who could enter and eat me at any given time? No.

Mira buried her head into her knees and clenched her fists. A rush of sadness came upon her. Mira began to cry. If she ever found a way to leave that lair, she promised, deep in her heart, that she would never take anything for granted ever again.

"I haven't been the best person lately," Mira said aloud, admitting to her faults. "No wonder Bash sold us out to the monster. I was so mean to him." Mira went on whispering solemnly to herself. "But I'm going to do better... once I get out of here."

Emboldened by her remorse, Mira stood up from her little corner and walked over to the tall bars that enclosed the cell determined to find a way out. She reached her hand through and tried to squeeze her body out between the bars. She failed. Mira went back to her corner to plot another way to escape, but so many depressing thoughts filled her head.

Why hasn't anyone come to get me? Mira asked herself. My friends from school probably aren't worried about me, and neither is Bash. Maybe because I always push people away.

Mira couldn't think straight. Discouraged, she knew that at the rate she was going, it would be a long while before she finally came up with another plan. A plan she didn't know would inevitably fail because the cell she was being held in was especially designed to keep even the smartest and strongest person from escaping.

CHAPTER 12

Standing outside the Apollyon's lair, Bash convinced himself of what he was about to do.

"Alright," he said, under his breath. "The twins had no choice but to fight the monster alone. They're probably captured by now, along with Mira. I have the book, so that's good. Now I need to come up with a plan to save the three of them."

Bash walked around for a good thirty minutes. In the field where his mother had sacrificed herself for him, Bash remembered how she used to go out of her way to help people survive on Pollutio. How can I help Mira, Kai, and Kam? Bash asked himself as he racked his brain, trying to come up with a plan to save his friends.

"That's it!" he exclaimed. "I'll wait until the monster is asleep, and then I'll pass by it and save them," Bash said.

Still being cautious, Bash collected his staff, nails, and a sheet of rusted metal to use as a shield to help protect himself in case the Apollyon was a light sleeper. When he finished collecting the items he needed, Bash headed for the monster's lair. He arrived at the mouth of the cave and crept a few inches inside as quietly as he could.

"Okay, the Apollyon is sleeping," Bash whispered to himself.

As he looked around his surroundings, Bash noticed a path and a ring of keys. Bash put his thieving skills to use and snagged the keys stored in the Apollyon's collection piles where he had taken the book of lost magic earlier. With the keys safely in his possession, Bash decided to follow the path. He spied to see where it led. As he walked, he saw rows of cells that seemed to go on forever.

"Dang, this cave is huge," Bash said quietly in surprise.

Wandering down the path, Bash finally saw Mira and the twins.

"Bash, you came to save us!" Mira screamed.

Mira was happy to see Bash, but the twins were not. "His conscience was probably eating him up," Kai muttered. "That's the only reason he came back."

Mira looked around, confused.

"Oh, yeah, we didn't tell you how we also got captured," Kam chimed in. "Our lovely friend Bash decided to leave us to the Apollyon so he could steal the book for himself."

Mira looked at Bash in disbelief. Upset by what she'd just heard about him, it didn't outweigh the fact that she was still happy to see him.

"Guys, I'm sorry," Bash began. "But I wanted to make sure you guys were okay, so I came back. Let's go before the Apollyon wakes up."

Bash took his staff and nails he had armed himself with just outside the Apollyon's lair. He noticed that around him on the ground were Kai's shattered sword and Kam's bow and quiver full of arrows. He smiled, picked up Kam's bow and arrows, and handed them to her.

"Kai and Kam, I got your weapons back," Bash said with a smile.

Using the keys he swiped from the Apollyon's collections, Bash released Mira, Kai, and Kam. Finally free, instead of thanking him, Kai and Kam snatched their weapons and walked past Bash, intentionally bumping his shoulders to make him fall.

"Thanks, Bash," Mira said in a quiet, timid voice. Even though she was hurt that Bash had left them to die, she believed he couldn't have done it for no reason.

"I'm so sorry, again." Bash apologized as Mira, Kai, and Kam walked away from him. "I really don't know what came over me."

"I do," Kam said, whirling around. "Greed and selfishness."

Bash stayed silent because he couldn't argue with the facts. As the four of them walked back to the entrance of the cave, it seemed to Bash like it was darker than when he first entered.

"Guys, something is off. Be ready for anything," Bash warned as the foreboding feeling settled deep within him.

"Last time you said that, you ran off," Kai mocked.

They kept walking until they reached the place where the monster was supposedly sleeping.

"Ha ha ha," he laughed, leaping to his feet. "So you came to take away my breakfast, lunch, and dinner?" the monster asked Bash through an angry smile.

The group, confused by the monster's mismatched reaction, drew their weapons, ready to attack.

"Okay, Mira, stay behind me," Bash ordered. "Kai and Kam, I want you guys to help me surround Mira and protect her, but also protect yourselves. The monsters of Pollutio all have the same weak spot between their eyes."

"Perfect. Thanks for the information," Kai said, running toward the monster at full speed and swinging his sword.

Kai missed landing the first strike of his sword, but he tried again, never letting down his guard.

"I can't reach the eye! It's too tall," Kai yelled to Kam and Bash.

"Kam, protect Mira," Bash said.

He went for the attack with his rusted staff and punted its sharpened javelin tip toward the Apollyon's eye. But it was just too far. The spear hit the side of the cave.

"It's my turn now," Kam said. Standing guard in front of Mira, she pulled an arrow out of the quiver she had slung across her back and focused her aim on one of the Apollyon's long bejeweled eyes.

She coached herself. "Steady, steady, and... bullseye!"

Kam successfully hit the monster in the eye. The Apollyon doubled over in pain and yelped, "You dumb kids! How dare you hurt me."

The Apollyon screamed in agony, but still with that weird smile that seemed almost painted on its face.

"Let's go! Hurry up, while it's distracted," Mira yelled in amazement at all the brave fighting that had taken place. What she had seen was something she'd normally only watched in movies, but now she had witnessed it in real life. Together, Mira, Bash, Kai, and Kam ran out of the cave as fast as they could and headed back to Bash's hut.

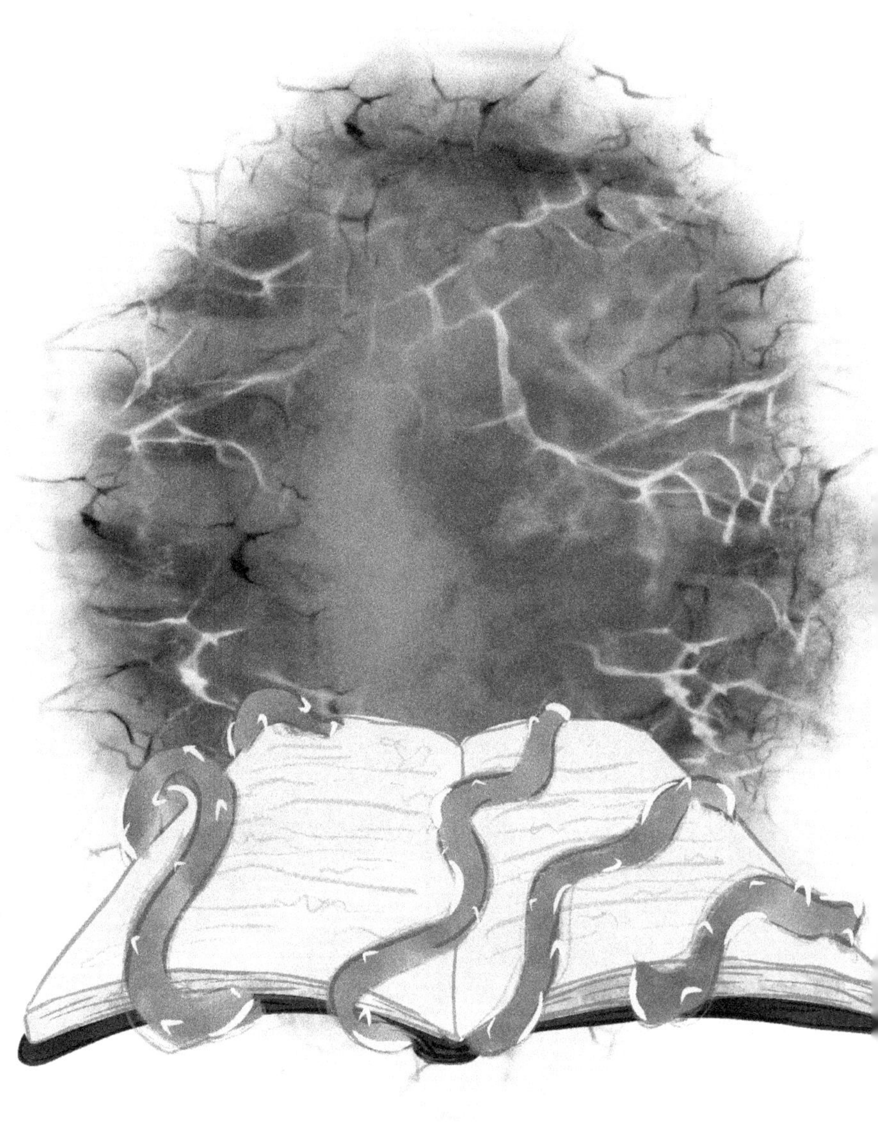

CHAPTER 13

Everyone cheered.

"Whooo! We did it," Kai screamed excitedly.

But despite the jubilant voices the atmosphere was still filled with the tension from Bash's betrayal.

"I just want to say that I'm still very sorry for what I did," Bash said, sensing the mood. "I know it —"

"Bash, we aren't mad at you. Just a little hurt," Kam said, cutting him off. "But of course we are happy that you decided to come back for us."

Kam flashed her brightest smile to let Bash know that she meant what she said. Kai moved in for a hug, sensing that Bash was hurting and that was what had made him take the book of lost magic. Mira followed the twins and wrapped her arms around Bash, too. It was a group hug among the four of them, all of them happy that they had made it out alive and away from the monster's lair.

"Now let's open up this book and see how to get you guys home," Bash said, pumped.

"How, umm, do we use this thing?" Mira asked, confused.

Bash looked at Mira and then at the book. "Well, you see, I know about the book, but not really how to use it, but let's see," he said bashfully.

Bash flipped through the book, looking for any clue on how to activate its magic. Going through page after page, Bash finally found a puzzle that had to be drawn out to reveal a portal. But it was incomplete.

"We were so close," Kai wailed. "How are we supposed to find the other piece of the puzzle now? We are never going back home."

"Is nothing else in there?" Kam asked. "Make sure."

"I'm sure," Bash said, flipping through the book once again to make sure he didn't miss anything.

Kai turned around in despair and banged his head against the wall of the hut.

"Wait!" Bash exclaimed. "Kai, what is that on the back of your head? Kam, do you have the same birthmark too?"

"Yes. Why?" Kam asked curiously.

"Hold on—can you turn around for me, next to your brother?" Bash asked.

Bash held up the book and saw that the book's puzzle connected to the birthmark on the backs of the twins' heads. "You guys complete the book. It's a match!"

Bash jumped up and down with excitement. The twins turned back around to face him. Confusion was written all over their faces.

Kam spoke first. "But we have never been here before. How can that be?"

"Well, this book is the book of lost magic," Bash emphasized. "It comes from... I believe, a Kingdom called... Aeolus," Bash stammered.

"That is the name of our kingdom," Kai said.

"Well, let's draw this puzzle out," Mira finally spoke up. "Does it matter where we do it?"

Bash looked through the book again to see if there were any special instructions about how to draw out the puzzle to open the portal. "No, it just says to draw out the puzzle and the book is at your pleasure," Bash answered. "It also says make sure you name where you would like to go above the portal."

Mira grabbed a stick and drew out the puzzle as close as to the images in the book as she could, looking from the book to the twins' heads and back again.

"Okay, I'm done. Now—"

Before Mira could finish her sentence, a blue circle appeared before them with a small key inside of it.

"All we have to do now is turn the key and the portal door should open," Bash said.

Kam pushed Bash out of the way and turned the key himself. The blue circle turned into a door they could physically walk through, like the one they had first fallen through when they arrived in Pollutio.

"I can see the castle!" Kai said excitedly.

The four of them smiled at each other then slowly stopped until their smiles turned upside down.

"Thank you, guys, for teaching me and Kam how to be better friends and how to truly understand what it's like to be a normal human that has feelings,"

Kam said. "Now we can be better leaders to our people of Aeolus."

"Yes, thank you for being great friends," Kai said.

Kai and Kam bowed to Mira and Bash, but Bash stopped them.

He said, "No, thank you for forgiving me, even though I betrayed you."

Bash bowed lower than the twins had to show them even more respect. Mira followed his lead and bowed on the ground beside Bash.

"Come visit us, okay? With your portals or something." Mira tried to laugh to keep the twins from seeing the tear rolling down her face.

Mirroring Mira, the twins laughed, too, then stood to their feet. Mira and Bash gave Kai and Kam one last hug before they said their goodbyes.

"Farewell, our friends," Kai and Kam said in unison.

Home at last, the twins thought to each other, happy that their telepathy powers were back to working at full strength.

CHAPTER 14

The twins were gone, and it was down to just two—Mira and Bash. They were as silent as a mouse as they looked around everywhere but at each other. Still uncomfortable, Bash spoke first.

"Mira, I know it has been very rough here, and I'm sorry you got caught by the monster because of me..."

Mira turned her face away from Bash. He stopped speaking as she made little gasps. Bash shuffled to see her face. When he did, he realized she was crying.

"I'm really sorry. I didn't mean to make you upset," Bash said, tripping over his words as they came out of his mouth.

"Bash, I'm not mad at you. I'm sad that I have to leave you. I have to go back to my reality... that's hard for me." Mira said.

Bash reached out to give Mira a hug. "Don't worry. You can visit me anytime you want to because now we know how the portal works," he said. "You are welcome to come to Pollutio anytime." Bash smiled as big as the sun.

"Thank you, Bash. This was a very great experience, and I will be coming back."

Mira and Bash said their last goodbyes, then Bash used the book to open the portal back to Earth for Mira.

"Bye, Bash! See you later," Mira yelled after stepping inside.

She didn't hear if Bash said anything back to her. Mira was back on Earth and in the same place she was before she had left—on the field trip in the gardens of the Cummer Museum. Mira headed back toward her group that she had run from before.

"It's Mira, guys! She's back!" one classmate yelled.

The group came running toward Mira.

"Mira, we were so scared! We were looking for you everywhere. Are you okay?" another classmate asked.

Mira, feeling guilty, tried to hold back her tears. "I'm sorry, guys. I was being very selfish and bratty and not caring about everyone's opinions. I feel bad. I'm sorry."

A single tear ran down Mira's face. Her classmates surrounded her even more and tried to comfort her with their closeness.

"It's okay, Mira. We were more worried about you than what happened earlier," one said.

"Don't worry about it. It's all in the past," another classmate stated.

Mira wiped her face and smiled. "Thank you, guys, for being my classmates. Let's make the rest of this trip a good one."

Mira walked back toward the gardens with her friends to enjoy the rest of their trip, finally understanding why it was so important to listen to others.

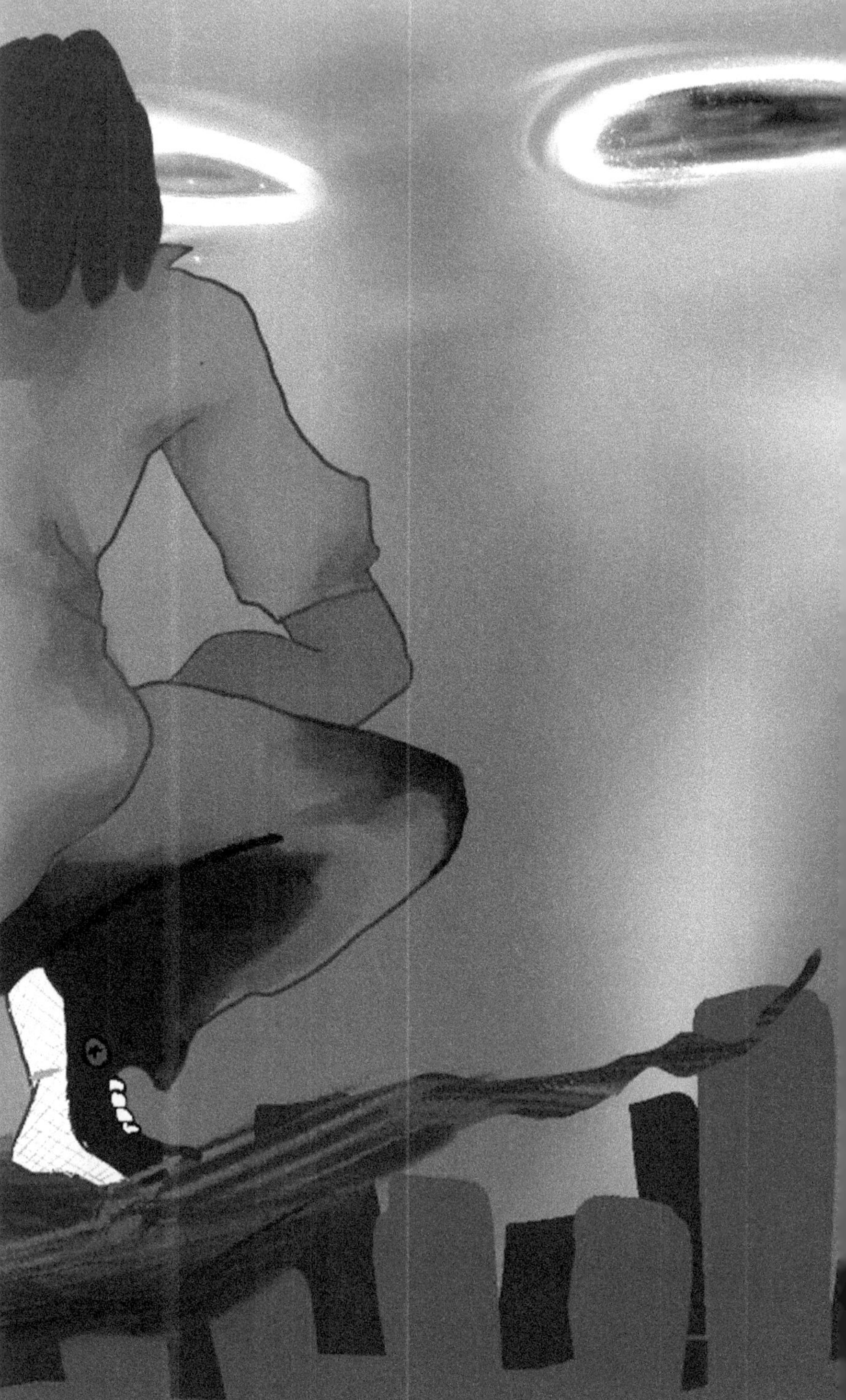

Acknowledgements

Jacksonville Arts & Music School (JAMS) is a creative arts and youth leadership focused after-school program whose mission is to empower the creative leaders of tomorrow. Special thank you to the students of House Savage, our visual arts department named in honor of Augusta Savage; Director of Education & Visual Art Instructor, Erin Kendrick; JAMS Writer-in-Residence and publisher, Nikesha Elise Williams; and The Cummer Museum of Art & Gardens Education, Gardens, and Marketing Staff.

Kim Kuta Dring, Director of Learning & Engagement
Patrick MacRae, Director of Gardens & Horticulture
Dulcie Hause, Asst. Director of Learning & Engagement
Karl Boecklen, Adult Programs Manager
Dima Kroma, Youth & Family Programs Manager
Craig Whitlock, Graphic Designer & Marketing Specialist

www.ingramcontent.com/pod-product-compliance
Lightning Source LLC
Chambersburg PA
CBHW070837020826
48982CB00021B/1409/J
* 9 7 8 1 7 3 5 7 2 1 9 6 5 *